Dear Parents:

Congratulations! Your child is taking the first steps on an exciting journey. The destination? Independent reading!

STEP INTO READING® will help your child get there. The program offers five steps to reading success. Each step includes fun stories and colorful art or photographs. In addition to original fiction and books with favorite characters, there are Step into Reading Non-Fiction Readers, Phonics Readers and Boxed Sets, Sticker Readers, and Comic Readers—a complete literacy program with something to interest every child.

Learning to Read, Step by Step!

Ready to Read Preschool–Kindergarten
• big type and easy words • rhyme and rhythm • picture clues
For children who know the alphabet and are eager to begin reading.

Reading with Help Preschool–Grade 1
• basic vocabulary • short sentences • simple stories
For children who recognize familiar words and sound out new words with help.

Reading on Your Own Grades 1–3
• engaging characters • easy-to-follow plots • popular topics
For children who are ready to read on their own.

Reading Paragraphs Grades 2–3
• challenging vocabulary • short paragraphs • exciting stories
For newly independent readers who read simple sentences with confidence.

Ready for Chapters Grades 2–4
• chapters • longer paragraphs • full-color art
For children who want to take the plunge into chapter books but still like colorful pictures.

STEP INTO READING® is designed to give every child a successful reading experience. The grade levels are only guides; children will progress through the steps at their own speed, developing confidence in their reading.

Remember, a lifetime love of reading starts with a single step!

Published in the United States by Random House Children's Books, a division of Penguin
Random House LLC, 1745 Broadway, New York, NY 10019, and in Canada by Penguin Random
House Canada Limited, Toronto.

Step into Reading, Random House, and the Random House colophon are registered trademarks of
Penguin Random House LLC.

Visit us on the Web!
StepIntoReading.com
rhcbooks.com

Educators and librarians, for a variety of teaching tools, visit us at RHTeachersLibrarians.com

ISBN 978-0-593-31045-8 (trade)
ISBN 978-0-593-31046-5 (lib. bdg.)
ISBN 978-0-593-31047-2 (ebook)

Printed in the United States of America

10 9 8 7 6 5 4 3 2 1

STEP 3

STEP INTO READING®

READING ON YOUR OWN

THE BATMAN

by David Lewman
illustrated by Patrick Spaziante

Batman created by Bob Kane with Bill Finger

Random House 🏠 New York

Batman wants to make
Gotham City a safe place.
He watches over the city,
always on the lookout
for bad guys and villains.

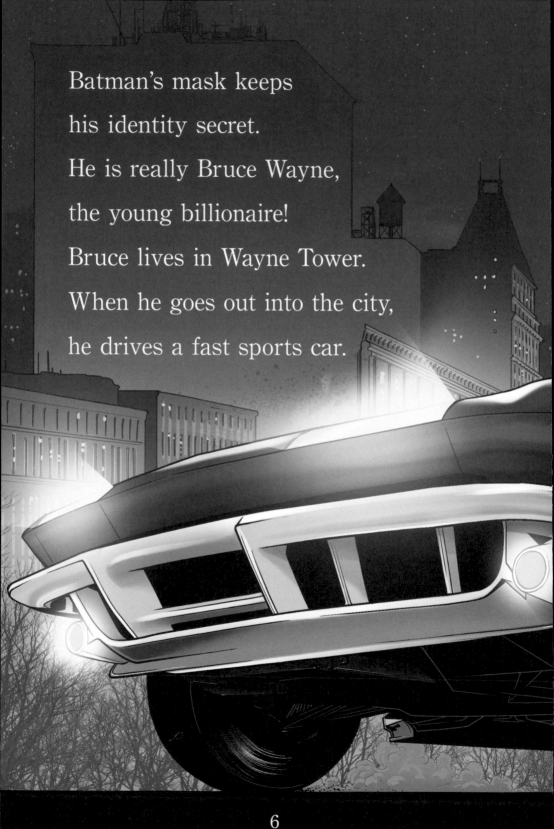

Batman's mask keeps
his identity secret.
He is really Bruce Wayne,
the young billionaire!
Bruce lives in Wayne Tower.
When he goes out into the city,
he drives a fast sports car.

But every night,
Bruce patrols Gotham City
looking for criminals.

He dresses in disguise
so no one will notice him.
He carries his Batman suit
in a backpack.
He is ready to change into it
whenever someone needs help!

Bruce rides his motorcycle
through an old tunnel
no one else uses.
The tunnel leads
to his headquarters.

Batman's secret headquarters
are under Wayne Tower.
He designs gadgets and uses computers
to help him solve crimes.

He works on a car
with a powerful engine.
He calls it the Batmobile.

VROOOOM!

Batman roars through
the streets of Gotham City.
No criminal can get away
from the Batmobile.
It's too fast!

The only person who knows
Batman's real identity
is his butler, Alfred.

Alfred is more than a butler.
He is good at cracking
secret codes and helping
Batman on his missions.

Lieutenant James Gordon
is a police detective.
He knows Batman is
brilliant at solving crimes.

Lieutenant Gordon
lets Batman visit
crime scenes
to help find clues.

When Lieutenant Gordon
needs Batman's help,
he lights the Bat-Signal.
Batman can see it shining
from anywhere in the city.
He comes right away!
Criminals run and hide
when they see it.

Selina Kyle also wants
to clean up Gotham City.

She knows where all
the crooks like to meet.
They don't realize
that Selina is . . .

...CATWOMAN!

Catwoman is
a martial arts expert.
She is more than a match
for the city's bad guys.

Oswald Cobblepot is a crime boss who is always up to no good.
He wants people to call him Oz.
He thinks it sounds cool.
Instead, they call him The Penguin.
He does NOT like that!

But there is an even
more dangerous
bad guy on the loose—
The Riddler!

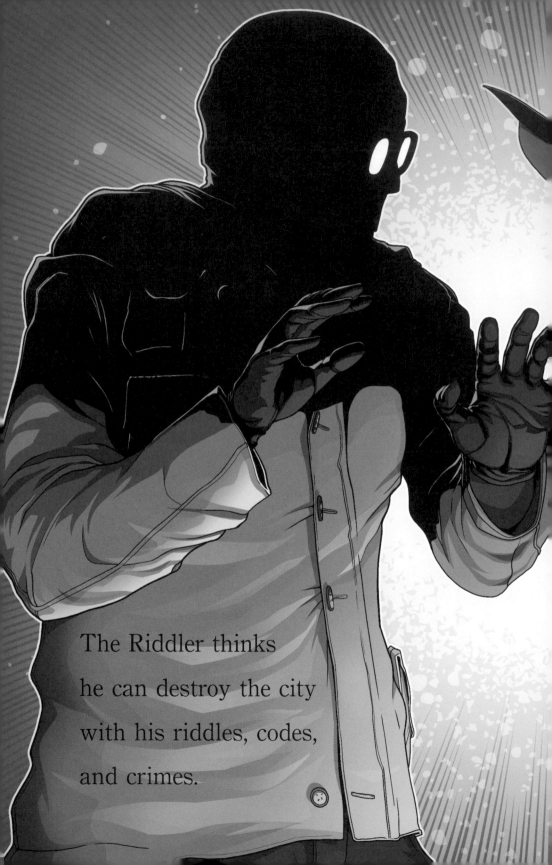

The Riddler thinks he can destroy the city with his riddles, codes, and crimes.

Batman and Catwoman
team up!

With Catwoman's help,

Batman catches The Riddler!

Lieutenant Gordon is grateful
for the mysterious crime fighters.

Gotham City is safe
as long as Batman
has good people
helping him protect it!